Respectfully Yours

A Compilation of Musing Moments

by

Veronica Moore

AKA - Fay Ferguson

authorHOUSE®

AuthorHouse™
1663 Liberty Drive, Suite 200
Bloomington, IN 47403
www.authorhouse.com
Phone: 1-800-839-8640

©2009 Veronica Moore. All rights reserved.

No part of this book may be reproduced, stored in a retrieval system, or transmitted by any means without the written permission of the author.

First published by AuthorHouse   3/23/2009

ISBN: 978-1-4343-6715-0 (sc)

Library of Congress Control Number: 2008901580

Printed in the United States of America
Bloomington, Indiana

This book is printed on acid-free paper.

DEDICATION:

I thank God, our Almighty Creator, for his inspiration. I dedicate this book to my parents, and teachers.

ACKNOWLEDGEMENT:

Much appreciation goes to my family and friends - in alphabetical order - for their support. Special mention goes to Howard Moore (II), Karen Malcolm, Martin Russell, Nadine Raymond, Natalie Moore and Sharon Lakhan.

CONTENTS

Introduction	WHAT'S IN A POEM	1
1.	GIFTS IN POETRY	3
	A Friend	
	A Little Gentleman	
	Birthday Roast	
	Chant For A Chap	
	For Grandma	
	Frustration	
	Mother's Wisdom	
	Our Son	
	To A Little Miss	
2.	IN MEMORY	17
	Dedicated	
	Letter To A Lady	
	Patience Is A Virtue	
3.	MUCH MUSING	23
	America The Brave	
	Chakras	
	Comeback Jamaica	
	Dabbling	
	Dreaming	
	Empathy For Mikey	
	If I Could, I Would	
	Sleep	

4. **PONDERING IN POEMS**   39
   God's Breath
   Lonely Starlight
   Our Companion
   Our West
   Reflections
   Rhythm In Life
   Trees
   Who We Are

5. **ROMANTIC BLUES**   53
   Back With Mike
   Body, Mind and Spirit
   Entrepreneur Of Love
   Giant Memories
   Ode To Michael
   You Don't

6. **SCENERY IN POETRY**   65
   Along The Trail
   Bona Vista
   City Sirens
   Flock At The Dock
   Good Bye, P.E.I.
   Jolly Joe
   The Park
   Writing On The Wall

7. **TALES IN POETRY**   81
   Family Woe
   Live Evil
   Picnic Puzzle
   Snow Dove
   Stay Awhile
   The Stranger

8.	VOCATIONAL VOICE		95
	An Adjuster's Jingle		
	Comrades		
	One Sixty Four		
9.	PUNS AND JESTERS		105
	Logo For Letterhead		
	New Dad		
	Pilot's Corner		
	Wedding Gift		

Meanings   111
References   119

PHOTOGRAPHS:

The pictures were designed from items in the home.
Some pictures were cropped and edited by the Author

1	Cover	Picture taken by the Author
2	Poems	Picture taken by the Author
3	Teddy	Picture taken by the Author
4	In memory	Picture taken by the Author
5	Outdoors	Picture at Hope Gardens (Jamaica) taken by the Author
6	Poinciana	Picture of Poinciana Tree at Hope Gardens (Jamaica) taken by Nadine Raymond
7	Rose	Picture taken by the Author
8	P.E.I.	Picture of a souvenir plaque from PEI and taken by the Author
9	Pets	Picture of a relative's wall décor taken by Nadine Raymond
10	Beach	Picture at Hellshire Beach (Jamaica) taken by the Author
11	Zoo	Picture of a poster (by unknown artist) taken by the Author

"If words in rhythm and rhyme are soothing to the soul and mind, read on…give me the best of it".

Veronica Moore

WHAT'S IN A POEM

A blurb of blurbs
Or a bevy of words
In rhythm or in rhyme
Written line by line

May add shapes and sizes
Some may win prizes
A sentence or a phrase
Upon which to graze

Some punctuation here
A few adjectives there
An adverb if you choose
A metaphor and you can't lose

Not too lengthy an alliteration
Will add to your creation
A simple simile
Will add simplicity

You can tell a story
Or praise God in His glory
Watch your stanza
Herein lies your bonanza

Blend in some colour
With feeling and emotion
Maybe fact or maybe fiction
There is no conviction

Your thought and expression
Will give an impression
To the reader of your poem
And you hope they enjoy 'em

September 2007

GIFTS IN POETRY

A Friend
A Little Gentleman
Birthday Roast
Chant For A Chap
For Grandma
Frustration
Mother's Wisdom
Our Son
To A Little Miss

A FRIEND

Someone with whom you choose to play
Doll house and hide-and-go-seek,
Or hot-bread-and-butter and dodge ball.
You leave home early for school,
Then stop to wait and now you are late.
But for your friend you take the fall.
You both drag a bottle cap under your feet
On the smooth surface of the concrete
Your Teacher asks, "Who did that?"
And you looked at her and asked, "Did what?"
Then you both run off to have a good laugh.

Someone with whom you take turns
To screech your nails on the black chalk board
With faces as serious as judges.
Later you hide pictures in your book
Of your favourite television or movie stars
And sneakily pass them to your friend
Then suddenly your eyes make four
With the Teacher's dirty look.
Now you have to stand in the classroom
In the usual time out nook.

Your friend lives far away
So at the railway station you stay
Using these valuable moments to catch up
On everybody's daily gossip.
You are tardy getting home after school
Now to meet your mother's beating stick.
A friend is someone to visit unexpectedly
And get chased by the dog
Who was sleeping soundly - you thought
But picked up you scent as you tiptoed by.

You ran - dashed - hoping to reach
The door around the back
But too late, he is on your heel
So through the window you jump
Not knowing what's on the other side of the wall
Luckily, a bed - with a sleeping baby on it
Fortunately there was room for you to fit
Thankfully! No harm done.
Your friend will pick you up or drop you off
To medical appointments or dates
To a party or a private place
Where your family is not welcomed.
A friend is someone you can laugh with
Or cry on, and share special moments;
Or ask you for a loan and pay you back
With interest on your dollars and cents.
Your friend is there through
Good times and bad, happy or sad,
High and low or thick and thin
Lose or win, your friend to the very end.
_____.

October 2007

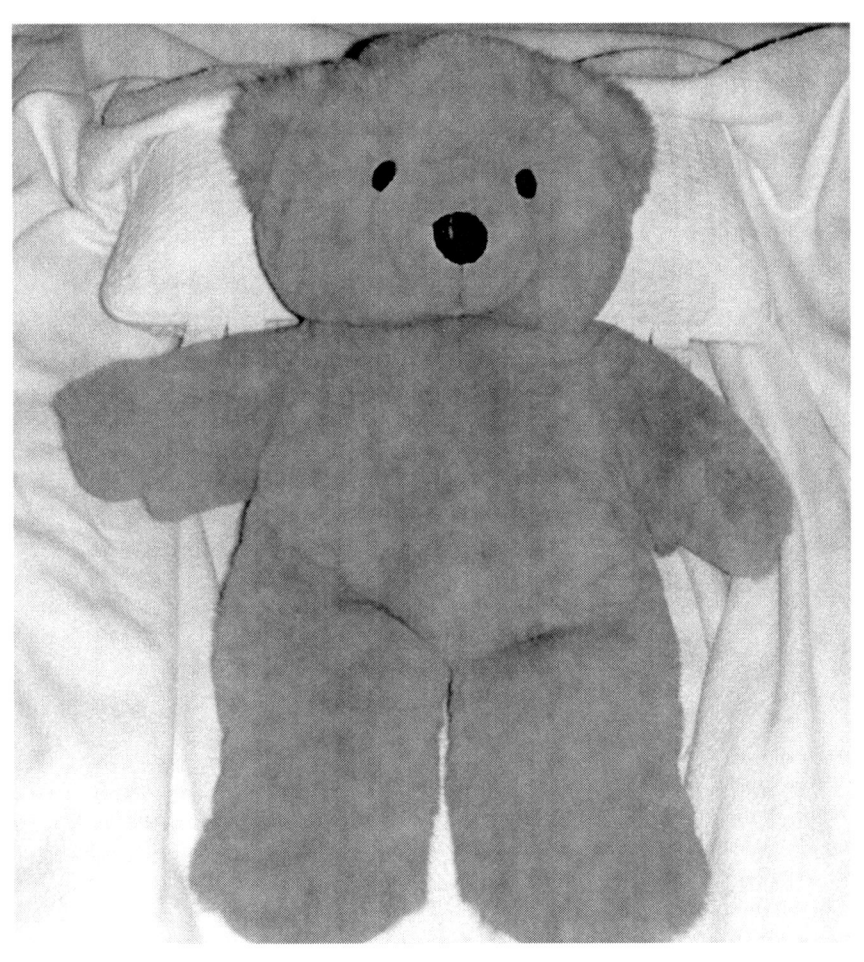

A LITTLE GENTLEMAN

Goodness gracious, Dylan turns eight.
This is absolutely great!
To see him growing bigger and taller,
Making grandma look so much smaller.

He is now coming into his own
And will reap from the good things that he has sown.
Things such as reading, math and spelling
He will be brilliant, there is just no telling.

He will soon outgrow his childhood ailments
And be much relieved from the air in the vents
He can win this battle with good eating habits
Such as fresh fruits and vegetable sticks.

He will take no food colorings in his diet
So that he will find some peace and quiet,
And become the perfect little gentleman
Who will take care of his female clan.

They are Sister,
Mommy and Grandma,
His three dearest of the female species,
Who will dote on him for all eternity.

~~~~~~~~~~~~~~
August 2006

BIRTHDAY ROAST

There is a little lady nicknamed "W".
Some people say, "she little, but she *'tallawah'*"
And if you don't trouble *ar*, she won't trouble *yu*.
"W" has a memory like an elephant
Her brain cells are most definitely not stagnant.
Some folks at seventy-five are already senile;
Not "W"! She can turn a frown into a smile.

She is generous, strong-willed, and she *care*.
When she opens her big round eyes and gives us the stare
We know we have something to fear.
She would fling the slippers and grab the broomstick,
But to chase seven children, she wasn't that quick.
Father, in his joyful mood, would call her *'Mother Mizza'*
But we leave that one between them, *yah sah*!
We call her a good, fun-loving mother
Washer, cleaner, sewer, cook, et cetera,
Since we never once go to bed without supper.

Next day after we finished school,
Behind the Town Library we went to play.
Now, keep in mind that 'W' is no fool.
Who did we glimpse rushing along the way?
Nu "W" with the strap flashing in her hand
Like a Fairy God Mother waving her magic wand.
Some of us got caught as the strap reached our butts
We scampered, grabbing books and grips like we were nuts.

She is a mother to nieces, nephews, in-laws and friends.
Into her home, abundance the Lord always sends.
We are glad to have her with us,
Seventy five years on this earth
With all seven children to whom she gave birth.
May the Lord continue to bless her
Until that day when he calls her to rest.

~~~~~~~~~~~~~~~~~~~

November 2004

CHANT FOR A CHAP

      You cared
          You loved

    A listening ear
        You always had

    You respected
          And never rejected

Those who crossed your path
          Aye! The richness of your heart

    Alas! You are ill,
        Confined to being so still

You said that age did not matter
        At ninety, you could still be a starter

You always thought on the positive side.
        The Lord will forever be your guide.

****

March 1996

FOR GRANDMA

Fearless
Always on the ball
You're pretty

Very good at poems
Ever lasting love
Really healthy
On the ball
Never not neat
I like her
Cool
Awesome

You
Real rich
Grandmother
Ongoing
Nice forever
Sings row, row, row your boat
You like to perm hair
Happy Birthday!

By Andi Raymond
~~~~~~~~~~~~~~~~
July 2006

FRUSTRATION

Sister, leave them now.
      You have taught them,
And showed them how.

Your daughter is seven
      Your sons are now
Twelve and eleven.

They are babies no longer
      But with each day, grow stronger
To adapt, and to learn that

Towards their future, they will earn
      The reaping of their sowing
Throughout their daily coming and going.

Sister, you must save your breath
      And guide them in their choices.
They will send you to an early death

Since what's pleasing to them
      Are their own demanding voices,
Their numerous video games,

And calling each other names;
      Not homework, nor school books
But to give each other rivalry looks.

They will eventually see the need
      To be the best siblings they can be.
Leave them now, Sister.

~~~~~~~~~~~~~~~

September 2007

MOTHER'S WISDOM

Read the Bible

You will have knowledge,
wisdom and understanding.

Always pray and work,
because prayer and work conquer all.

Spend wisely; you earned your income,
why waste your outgo.

Plan your future,
it is either retirement or death.

Eat wisely,
you become what you eat.

Live well,
life is a precious gift.

Have lots of fun,
it will make you laugh light-heartedly.

Give generously,
but never be taken for granted.

Forgive yourself and others,
it relieves a burdened spirit.

Love with half your heart,
only a quarter will be broken.

It can never be broken in two;
and remember that

I will always love you.

,,,,,,,,,,,,

April 1999

"OUR SON"

He saw, he loved, he conquered her heart.
She, one of three, from whom he will not soon part.
First in line, was she who bred and nurtured him.
I would have awarded her the golden pin.

With her love, she did lather;
And taught him that love must be shared with another.
To know him, is knowing that she would have been proud;
Alas! Fate and destiny clothed her in a shroud.

The second, he sought after, she being my daughter;
Did not know then, she was being lured to the lion's den.
For his day he celebrates under the star of Leo
Both unaware they would soon become a 'trio.

Ah! Ah! Here comes number three, precious little Andi
Who, very soon, will be calling me 'Grandi.'
Sad! Because she will have only one grandma of two;
Now twice the load I'll carry, to love them all so true.

....
August 1996

TO A LITTLE MISS

You are cuddly and cute as a bunny
Your richness will go beyond money
You are as elegant as the flamingo
As you peer outside of the window.

You want to be a veterinarian
Who treats and cares for animals
You are such a humanitarian
But be careful, some can be cannibals.

You light up the world with your smile
And you are far from being docile
You will ace all subjects in school,
Simply because you love to rule.

A bit more patience will go a long way.
To listen more will crown your day.
You will become everyone's best friend
For in every crowd you know how to blend.

As you grow and mature, naturally
You will be the envy of every family
Who wants their grand daughter
To be full of joy and laughter.

Happy Birthday
Is what I meant to say.

~~~~~~~~~~~~~~~~~~~~~.

July 2006

IN MEMORY

    Dedicated
    Letter To A Lady
    Patience Is A Virtue

DEDICATED
(Norma – May 10, 1949 to November 29, 1999)

She taught me how to pray
Alleluia, Alleluia, I say
I could hear throughout the house
Not the stirring of a mouse
But songs and prayers from her lips
And hand-clapping through to her fingertips.

She would 'waken in the early morn'
And praise God that she has seen the dawn,
The grass, the flowers and trees that grow;
Or even a cold winter morning of ice and snow.

At dusk, from work she would quietly creep in,
Turning the key while praying for a blessing
And thanking The Lord whom she did so adore;
She would enter in and praise Him some more.

In her faith, she showed much pride
And retired with her Bible by her side
Now, in my coming and my going, I do the same
I know, with the Lord Almighty, she has fame.

....
December 1999

LETTER TO A LADY
(Lady Diana - July 1, 1961 to August 31, 1997)

Dear Lady 'Di',
You were so very shy
As you glanced timidly through sky blue eyes,
And waved graciously, your royal good-byes.

Tall, elegant and slender
Pale, delicate and tender;
A Queen's title you will never gain,
But a Princess you'll always remain

In the hearts of the whole human race
Whom you charmed with love, beauty and grace.
Your precious sons, Princes William and Harry,
Your youthful memories they will always carry;

Fate and destiny can sometimes be unfair;
But you'll be remembered, free of wear and tear
'Cause though you're now so very cold
You will never ever grow old.

You were so very real, and not a fairy tale.
Had you been a virgin, you may have been crowned, 'Hail';
Like Cinderella, Snow White and Rapunzel,
Your name will forever ring a pleasant bell.

You have truly left your mark
As the Queen of our hearts;
Again, farewell to a Princess true,
Whose smile will forevermore, shine through.

~~~~~~~~~~~~~~~~~~~~~~~

September 1997

PATIENCE IS A VIRTUE
(Ivan – April 14, 1923 to November 19, 1983)

Mother would fling and give a cussing
While father would sing with no fussing

...Refrain...
"Patience is a virtue. If you have none of it,
It will hurt you.
If you have too much of it, it will hurt you
But you must have enough of it
To control yourself, for patience is a virtue."

So much time we spend in line
Waiting for the train, the bus, or the plane
Will it be here on time?
Checking your watch might drive you insane
So here we go again

...Refrain...
"Patience is a virtue. If you have none of it,
It will hurt you.
If you have too much of it, it will hurt you
But you must have enough of it
To control yourself, for patience is a virtue."

At the check-out counter and the instant teller
Suddenly! In front jumps a fellow
With your hand akimbo and lots of attitude
You tap him on the shoulder and say, "Man, you rude!"

...Refrain...
"Patience is a virtue. If you have none of it,
It will hurt you.
If you have too much of it, it will hurt you
But you must have enough of it
To control yourself, for patience is a virtue."

Your family irks you while your friends hurt you
You feel puzzled and don't know what to do
You want to pull out a gun, or fight with a knife
Stop! And think, because you have a life
No need to put yourself in a tizzy,
Lift your head high and get busy

...Refrain...
"Patience is a virtue. If you have none of it,
It will hurt you.
If you have too much of it, it will hurt you
But you must have enough of it
To control yourself, for patience is a virtue."

Take your job for instance, where you make a living
Where others take while you are always giving
Pulling your hair out while shuffling paper
Your boss leaves saying, 'See you later'
Your desk is a mess, and you are feeling the stress
Well pick up your briefcase, and join the rat race
Humming this tune straight to your place

...Refrain...
"Patience is a virtue. If you have none of it,
It will hurt you.
If you have too much of it, it will hurt you
But you must have enough of it
To control yourself, for patience is a virtue."

****

September 1997

MUCH MUSING

America The Brave
Chakras
Comeback Jamaica
Dabbling
Dreaming
Empathy For Mikey
If I Could, I Would
Sleep

AMERICA THE BRAVE

America, how we love thee
Yet despise thee in the same breath
You are the land of the brave and the free
But some wait for your sudden death
Your demise would be the annihilation
Of our democratic society
To you, may the Lord bestow guidance
And much prosperity

You have gained your place
In the race to Space
But for each space ship that leaves the earth
To more pollution they give birth
We have an ongoing love-hate relationship
But you must wake up and get a grip
You are tearing me apart
And so this is where I start

You delete negotiation from your vocabulary
And replace it with war and the military
I admire you from where you came
To build a nation into fortune and fame
A people brought from another Empire
Now other nation's dream and desire
Yet America, how did you achieve this
Befriending victims promising them bliss

Plundering, pilfering, buying slaves
Taking others' resources and replacing it with –
What's this?
Drafting, devastation and destruction
Victims wake up and realize they have been cheated
And vow that this will not be repeated
Some are disappointed America
In how you use your power

Wake up as a Christian nation to the Beatitudes
And remember the days of the Mayflower
Put away your arrogance, gluttony and greed;
Your unjust and seemingly selfish attitudes
Some say you are in others' back pockets
Some who say, "An eye for an eye,
And a tooth for a tooth"
Hang on, America, to your Christian root

We are all God's chosen people
Each nation under creation
Wake up America, before it's too late
Don't rule other nations
Bringing more enemies to your gate
Another's country is not your playground
Nor for you to pursue and hound
But focus on issues to your detriment

Not at the indiscretions of a President
While your enemies plot and plan
Consider your descendants
And the prosperity of your land
Still, America –
When all is said and done
We would rather live under your power
Than that of some other ones

///
October 2002

CHAKRAS

As the Earth provides a firm foundation,
So does my <u>base</u> chakra through its formation.
The lion in my constellation
Will be my representation.

The <u>sacral</u> that houses the testes and the ovaries -
Have been producing offspring for centuries.
As the sunflower put forth her seeds,
Each dew kiss petal will atone for my deeds.

The body is fed through the digestive system
Where the <u>solar plexus</u> lights up with fire.
The Sun keeps order with magnetic rhythm
A mighty life source of which I can't tire.

The <u>heart,</u> the fourth chakra of seven
Takes center stage straight up to heaven.
With love and harmony at its very core
Hearts! We should all be asking for more.

The <u>throat</u> down which all food goes,
And self expression is all it knows;
Blue-flamed fire which is my element -
Will purge all words before they are sent.

The <u>third eye</u> chakra, the mediator,
It oversees the soul and the personality.
The Cross for spirituality- the Son of the Creator
What other symbol carries such deity?

Last, but not least, the <u>crown</u> is number seven;
A holier number than six or eleven.
The divine creator used it time and time again
Perfecting all in three score and ten - divided by ten.

,,,,,,,,,,,,,,,,,,,,,,,,,,,,,,

April 2001

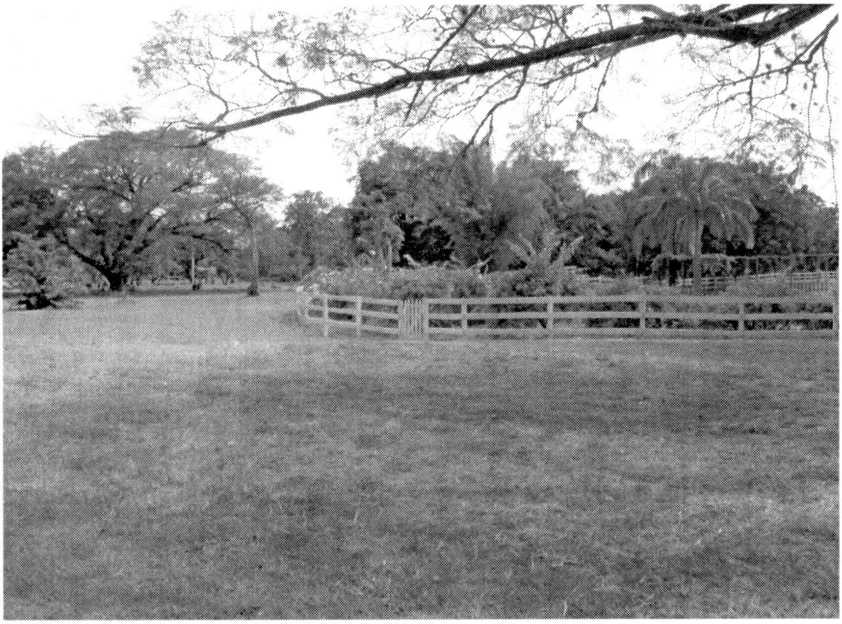

COMEBACK JAMAICA

What's happening, Jamaica?
Great land of wood and water
Many have crossed the seas
And have taken you to the slaughter

But you will forgive their prying
For in fact they are not lying
There used to be love and laughter
But now it's mostly disaster

With the spread of drugs and ammunition
And precious values gone astray
You have forgotten pride and ambition
And your brethren you now slay

Politicians, do they really care?
They have lost control for many a year
With their main concern
Being their own fair share

But Jamaica, you can turn around
And shame the critics to the ground
With your varied talents so widespread
And your knack for finding daily bread

*You range from the heights of Hollywood
To the ghettos of your neighbourhood
You are often times misunderstood
But in you there is still much good*

*So Jamaica! Remember decades ago
When life was not always so
Teach your children so they will know
That "Out of Many, One People"
Is still the best National Motto.*

~~~~~~~~~~~~~~~

March 1993

DABBLING

Dabble in that which is constructive
Like a bee building a hive

Dabble in that which is positive
Because it makes you feel alive

Dabble in that which is hope
It gives you the strength to cope

Dabble in that which is peace
Otherwise wars will never cease
It also puts your mind at ease

Dabble in that which is love
It was taught by the Lord above

Dabble in that which is true
And you will never feel blue

Dabble in that which is charitable
So you will always have food on your table

....

August 1994

DREAMING

We love our Black men
So strong, handsome and debonair;
But they seem to prefer other women
Who think they have only one flair.

Black men, look deep inside your souls -
What happened to education and vocation?
Communication and arts, culture and recreation
These too, are some of our goals.

You caress other women and father their kids;
You even push their shopping carts.
Take a second look! We're not invalids
And we too, have hearts.

We must now follow in your fashion
As your present treatment we abhor,
We must look in another direction
Where we can find someone to adore,

Shame on you Black men
For casting us aside.
Walk beside us and not behind us
In your great big black stride.
Together, we can still be each others guide.

Think again Black men -
Dignity, self-respect and self-esteem
Are innate qualities that you possess.
Don't ever believe that this is a dream;
These are issues that you must address.

,,,,,,,,,,,,,,,,,,,,,,,,,

February 1995

EMPATHY FOR MIKEY

I empathize with how you feel
As I sense that you are for real.
You love everyone - kids and all - from your heart;
Half the world is phony; the other half is an upstart.

They understand not what you are expressing;
See the Prosecutor's face during his questioning.
Oh! How depressing, as he tries to twist your words;
His eyes gleaming accusingly like sharp swords.

Why did you let them into your life
Why trust those who now stab you with a knife
You were doing fine with them just being curious;
Now they have made both me and you furious.

Today, following the rebuttal preview,
Newspapers, radio and television -
They say not one good thing about you.
If no 'Michael-bashing' - then no other session.

Our world, so dismal, that good news is passé
Only negativity they throw out our way.
Media, start sending the nations some good news;
Since positive energy our world could use.

~~~~~~~~~~~~~~~~~~~~~~~~~~~

February 2003

IF I COULD, I WOULD

If I could turn back the hands of time
Sure I would be the first one in line
To ask God that there be no sin
So we could be happy in The Garden of Eden.

If I could turn back the hands of time
I would ask God that there be no crime
No Eve, nor Cain, so that peace could reign
Love and unity would be our gain.

If I could turn back the hands of time
And God made me an angel divine
No way I would disobey, and be thrown in hell
To mingle with the likes of Delilah and Jezebel.

Neither money, nor power would I want to extort
From country, nor countryman - 'cause life is too short.
I know I could live and let others live,
And from my heart, much love I would give.

If I were brave and able to save some -
Like Kennedy, King, Marley and Malcolm,
Teresa, Diana, and yes, Clinton -
Then ask God to spare such inspiration.

If I could say to you all today…
We still have great ones, please let them stay
Without shame, and defame from their past.
Take the beam from your eyes, not from others', cast.

= = = = = = = = = = =

January 1998

SLEEP

Sleep, sleep, sleep
Oh, where art thou sleep?
You stay away -
And leave me counting
Sheep, sheep, sheep.

Oh, that you were my friend,
Longing to see me at day's end.
You stay away -
On account of these butterflies in my chest,
And deny me much rest, rest, rest.

I toss, I turn, the fluttering of my feet;
You are madly missed, sleep.
You stay away -
So I sit up and read, then count the
Sheep, sheep, sheep.

Sleep!
You deny me the sight of break of dawn.
You stay away -
So I miss the Sunrise and the early morn'
As you creep, creep, creep

Heavily upon my lanky limbs, my puffy lids.
You have now cast your spell;
You came to stay -
And now the world passes me by
As I drift into you - deep, deep, deep.

Come little lamb; come soon with your bell.
Come 'waken me before high noon that is nigh;
Sleep is here -
No more the need to count
Sheep, sheep, sheep.

`````````````````````````

September 2007
`````````````````````````

PONDERING IN POEMS

    God's Breath
    Lonely Starlight
    Our Companion
    Our West
    Reflections
    Rhythm In Life
    Trees
    Who We Are

GOD'S BREATH

A gentle breeze
Tells me that God is whispering to me,
To us - to the world.

A warm gentle breeze
Tells me that God is giving me a loving, caring hug.
His whisper is from his warmest breath.

A gentle rustle in the breeze
Tells me that God is walking quietly.
He approaches me. I am safe.

A great rustle in the breeze
Tells me that God is walking very fast.
He is in a hurry with great news. Listen world.

A strong breeze
Tells me that God is getting angry.
Pay attention.
What did I – we – the world do wrong?

Gale force breeze
Tells me that God is very angry.
He overthrows all in his path.
He makes the waters swell and rise.
Watch out world - take heed.

A cool gentle breeze
Tells me that God's anger is waned.
He is giving me – us – the world
Time to take action.
Now is our chance.

A cold breeze
Tells me that God is vexed and icy.
He breathes to freeze.

Dear God, don't let them take the trees
That produce the breeze
So that I – we – the world
Can feel your breath and forever hear your whisper.

````````````````````````````````````

November 2004
````````````````````````````````````

LONELY STARLIGHT

Lonely star high up above,
Twinkling down brightly with your love.

From the western corner of the sky
You tenderly shine upon Longmeadow,
Where the neighbours in their houses lie;
Their rooftops creating castles in your shadow.

As I closed the shutters over the window
I stood thoughtfully with hands akimbo
Stop! Open! Another look up to heaven
Only one lonely star, not seven, not eleven.

So still and lonely, but bright up there;
I keep staring, and am filled with fear
From that one and only, lonely star
So very bright, yet so very far.

It is surely looking back at me;
Like God's eye, it can see,
Guiding, guarding, and glistening,
It glared, I stared, my ears listening.

Overcome with curiosity, I decided to wink.
Sure enough, to be greeted with a blink
From that one and only, lonely starlight
Sitting atop the world to brighten the night.

****

May 1999

OUR COMPANION

Men, from whose ribs we came
Knew not what they had to gain
By having us by their side
Their true feelings they could hide

The companion bore the brunt of the pain
So that our men would not go insane
They are just like little boys
Who take us for one of their toys

With muscles hard, long and strong
Some feel they can do no wrong
But our constitution is stronger
And we do last so much longer

They vary in shape, height and size
And some, they are so very wise
We have them in bi, homo and hetero
Still! We always love them so

Some are brave, brawny and huge
And some come in a deluge
The Creator, he gave them a flat chest
For the companion, a perfect head rest

He also gave men flat tits
So that we would never be misfits.
So let's all pull up our socks
And count from one to ten

For the men, they are the peacocks
And we, the companion, are the hens.
....

March 1993

OUR WEST

Some say that the West
Was discovered in 1492
But no! There were indigenous
Long before Columbus, me and you.

The Arawaks in the Caribbean
Red Indians in the Northern Sphere
Take a look down South too,
They have straight, jet-black, long hair.

Then the pale ones came,
And Oh! What a shame!
They fought, burned and shot
And changed everyone's lot.

They chopped and made obsolete
The trees are almost gone
They pollute and deplete
From dusk until dawn.

Who will be our heirs?
Our children and theirs.
What values have we left them?
They don't even say prayers.

What will be their destiny
With no work to earn a penny?
They sit at home with videos
'Cause it's unsafe to go outdoors.

But the West
It has been put to the test
Stop now! Give destruction a rest
Let Mother Nature and Father Time
Perform at their best.

....

March 1993

REFLECTIONS

Sometimes I sit in awe
And think of all the things I saw
Between the heavens up above
And the lowly earth below

I saw the bright yellow sun by day
Those times I ran outside to play
At night, I saw the light by moon
Realizing it would be bedtime soon

I saw the twinkling of the stars above
This started me thinking of my love
Then I saw an airplane zooming by
This gave me a great yearning to fly

I then decided to take a trip
Of course it was on a large cruise ship
Now you ask, "What did I see?"
The wide blue ocean, open to greet me

I took a stroll out into the field
Flowers, plants and trees it did yield
Such a variegation of green
The most beautiful shades I have ever seen

I took a drive upon the highway
Then stopped to watch traffic from atop a skyway
And as I stood in awe and wonder
My mind's eye saw many great things to ponder

....

March 1993

RHYTHM IN LIFE

Listen to the ticking of the clocks
Watch as the pendulum swings

Listen at the door as someone knocks
Or to the rhythm that a birdie sings

Hear the train trampling on its track
That particular sound always comes back

Watch the folks moving to the music
As the rhythm pounds some just can't refuse it

See the lightning before the thunder
Then listen to the resounding sound

Hear the beating of a drum
To which all the town's people run

The baby that is now due
And the rhythmic pain Mothers go through

Feel the rhythmic pulsing of the heart
Note the cycle that keeps the seasons apart

Your feet as they take a jog in the park
And your regular daily start

Then night comes and it gets dark
See the Sun in its usual place

While the planets orbit in space
Look at the Moon in its quarterly phase

On all these happenings we gaze
And know our world is a planned maze

....
September 2007

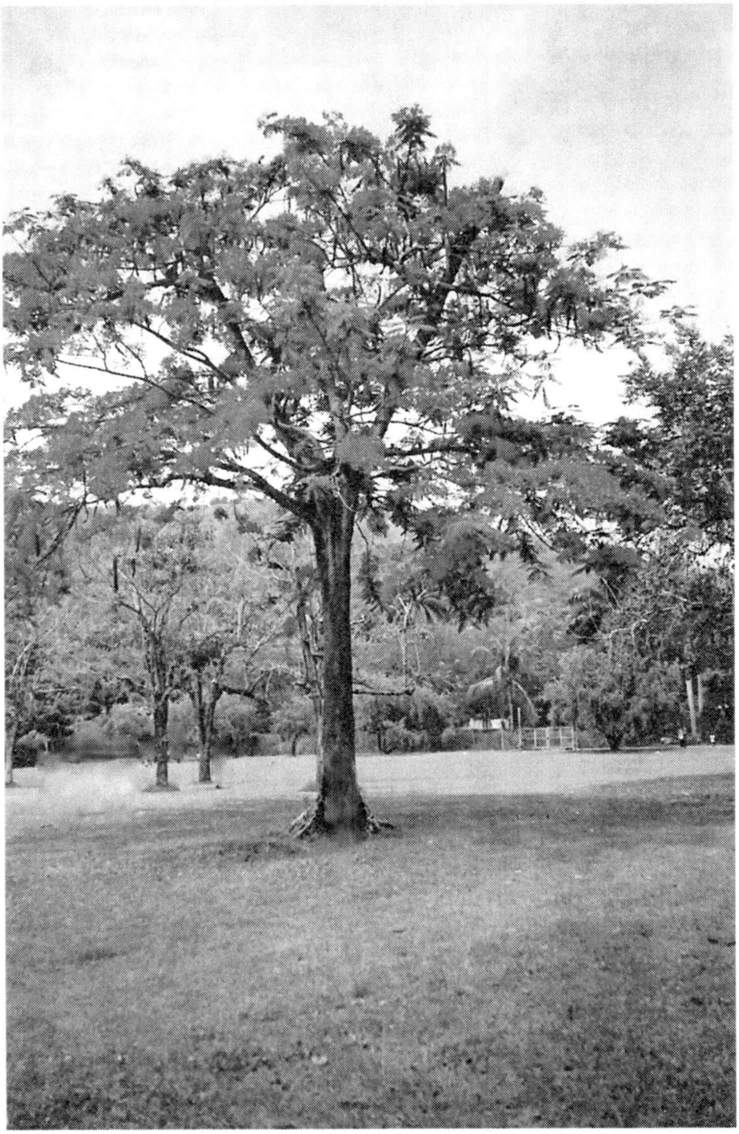

TREES

All year round
They sprout from the ground
Beautifying our glorious earth.
To seasons they give birth -
Naked and evergreen in winter
Fallen asleep are prickles and splinter.

Spring arrives and the trees are alive
With colours and flowers,
As sprouts and buds burst out
To the soaking of April showers.
Summer brings them to their peak -
Their tallest, widest and possibly driest.

Those will die, that are weak.
Those will remain that can stand the test.
Then comes the Autumn breeze,
Not so good for those with allergies;
Who do nothing all day but sneeze,
And talk about the colours of the Autumn leaves.

Trees secure the hills and mountain sides
And stop the avalanche and mud slides.
They are home to animals and birds of the wild;
And a rest-stop for a walker's pet and child.
They are nature's beauty and oxygen maker
Trees are carbon dioxide and smog taker.

....

September 2007

WHO WE ARE

He made us in His image
And in His likeness.
Why do we second guess
That our place is above the rest.
We are the superior beings.

Other life forms have their place
That is not superior to the human race.
Ours are wisdom, knowledge,
And understanding;
Then why are we unsettled

And wondering where we will live
Tomorrow, or into which hole
We should now burrow?
He will care for us
Like He does the sparrow.

We should not be fretting
For tomorrow,
Nor finding a home elsewhere.
This will be our sorrow;
Our forever, futile, furor -

To live somewhere up, up there
When we have it all
Down here, down here.
This place is where
We need to share and care.

==================
January 1997

ROMANTIC BLUES

Back With Mike
Body, Mind and Spirit
Entrepreneur Of Love
Giant Memories
Ode To Michael
You Don't

BACK WITH MIKE

I admired you just the way you were.
Your hair, your eyes, your lips
Your nose, your complexion -
All these, in their natural state, I miss.

The Good Lord may answer my prayer
To restore you to the way you were
And bring you into my lair.
Why did you make the transition

And put yourself in this position?
Do you not love yourself?
How can I have you
If you are a porcelain doll upon a shelf?

The media says you may lose your nose -
And what about your precious toes?
How will you again dance for me -
Your dance which I so love to see.

I will forever hold you in awe.
To me, you were perfect, without a flaw.
Our worlds being far apart; I could not coax you against it.
Promise that you will not make these changes a habit.

Nevertheless, I will always admire you.
Not your looks, or your treasury of varied talents;
But you are gentle, humane and true
If only all this made more sense!

∧∧∧∧∧∧∧∧∧∧∧∧

December 1997

BODY, MIND AND SPIRIT

He was a gift sent from heaven above,
To be her guide and to show her true love;
To guide her body, mind and spirit;
From his spirituality, she would benefit.

The evening whispered a cool summer breeze
Yet, their bodies were alight with a feverish fire.
They were able to dine and converse with ease
Their cheeks blushing with a burning desire.

Still, they could not deny what was ordained to be
As there were powers much mightier than he or she.
They were not meant to be together - often
But their pain; cherished memories will soften.

They were born to be tested,
Therefore, bodies, minds and spirits rested.
Past experience will be their great teacher;
Wearing the banner of friend, not partner, not preacher.

Be mindful that she is only human,
A mere mortal, a sensuous woman;
Being passionately impulsive was not so bad -
Why did life make her feel so sad?

He too, was made of flesh and blood.
Such self-restraint sets him aside as good
He was knowledgeable and had the right approach
Yet, this subject we should not broach.

Courage and understanding they will need
To exercise control throughout lust and greed,
And to endure those lonely days and nights -
These trials and tribulations will be their fights.

~~~~~~~~~~~~~~~~~~~~

February 2003

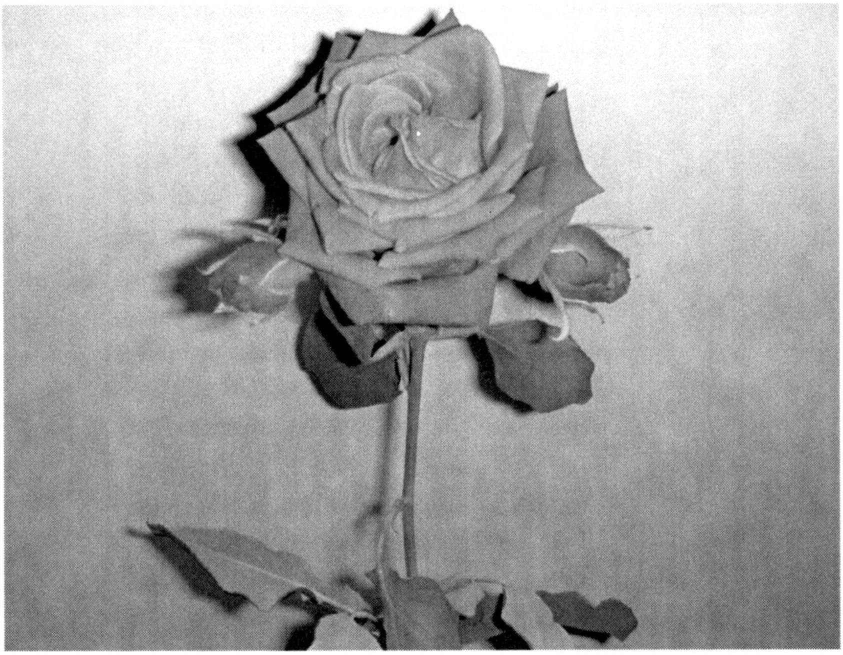

ENTREPRENEUR OF LOVE

Words never had to be said
And they never really needed a bed
For they had the chair, the floor and the stair
The entrepreneur of love is here

A seductive glance from he
A tantalizing touch from she
Would send them rolling around with glee
Lips searching and hearts pounding so free

Dressed to go, but bodies said, no!
Stay here awhile, let's toss to and fro
Their bodies entwined like cherubs above
She and the infamous entrepreneur of love

What they do to each other is unique
Now they're learning each others' technique
Doing it right - throughout the night
They'll never be out of each other's sight

Oh, yes! Oh, yes! She is a fast learner
With her one and only entrepreneur
Her web is spun and now he can't run
Their love has only just begun

Touch me, feel me, love me, and then some
All games have been played and now they're one
They are just like two peas in a pod
Because now, they're both entrepreneurs of love

~~~~~~~~~~~~~~~~

January 1998

GIANT MEMORIES

He is alias Mr. Broomfield
With her, he wears a shield
Standing tall at six feet, two
And most comfortable in a size eleven shoe

He is not a giant, but a man who walks among men.

He strides, a lethargic, bow-legged walk
Without which, he might have been the giant atop the beanstalk.
Peaceful and 'Gentle'; his name should have been 'Ben'
Minced meal he would be, if placed in a lion's den

He is not a giant, but a man who walks among men.

His subtle way with words
Used freely to bewitch the girls
Being humble and not one to gloat
He throws the ball right back in your court

He is not a giant, but a man who walks among men.

This lets him off the hook, I suppose
As he cunningly entices you to stop and smell the rose
His mind already made about the time and place
Where the bud he is surely going to taste

He is not a giant, but a man who walks among men.

The feline, from a long rest she was awakened
And now feeling desperately forsaken
Wondering if having gone Black
Will she truly be able to go back?

He is not a giant, but a man who walks among men.

~~~~~~~~~~~

August 1996

ODE TO MICHAEL

I love him
He is Michael

He is black
And he is white
I could cuddle him in the sack
And never let him out of my sight

Look how he moves and grooves
His feet like they are on heat
His lean body slithers here and there
His voice in a songful prayer

He is kind and very sensitive
Full of love and affection to give
To God's creatures great and small
And will rock them right 'off the wall'

He is truly 'the man in the mirror'
Full of grief and sorrow
But on stage you will never know it
For his performance is always a big hit

He is now getting out and about
Making folks scream and shout
He has a knack for perfectionism
But folks hound him with criticism

But nightly in my dreams
I protect him like a brother
From Brooke, Liz and Diana, it seems,
Wishing to steal him from under my cover

Here's hoping that some day
He will know that I care
'Cause in my heart, and in my own way
I know he's a dear
For his pain I do share

For I love him
He is Michael

****

March 1993

YOU DON'T

You are not the way you used to be.
You have so little time for me.
You say that you are far too busy;
Naturally, this leaves me in a tizzy.
Then I criticize you and you get bent,
And later scold me then remain silent.

You don't call or visit as you did before.
You probably think I am an insensitive bore.
You have that distant look in your eyes,
And your voice is as cold as ice.
You embrace me but you are very tense.
This is all not making any sense.

You don't make love as intense and as sweet.
You pulled the rug from right under my feet.
No loving dialogue before you are spent,
In my heart and mind you leave a dent
As you quietly drift off to sleep;
While I watch you in my pain, and weep.

You don't love me as in days gone by.
Please dear, I need you to tell me why.
You make promises that you do not keep;
Tell me if I am reading into this too deep.
You come back with excuses for a story;
Never mind dear, because you are history.

August 2002

SCENERY IN POETRY

Along The Trail
Bona Vista
City Sirens
Flock At The Dock
Good Bye P.E.I.
Jolly Joe
The Park
Writing On The Wall

ALONG THE TRAIL

(1)
Strolling along the trail
You risk kicking a pebble or two.
The trail is not rocky, or sandy or grassy;
Except on each side of the long winding trail,
Where the grass is sparse and frail.
Conducive to every type of shoe
Is the solid texture of cementy soil
Ranging from a hazy, smoke-grey
To a chalky slate-white sheet;
With some pebbles thrown in for a treat.
Where the absence of an asphalt surface
Causes no discomfort to the feet
No matter the temperature in the heat.

(2)
You cannot help but smile with other passersby
On this well walked winding trail,
Lined with picnic tables and food in abundance,
With music and drinks keeping folks in a trance.
Pets hobbling along, trying to lose leash and owner
And taking pit stops in their usual corner.
See the weeping willows like shredded scraps of cloth
Varying in length as they bow to the ground
Making that whispering, whimpering sound
As you stroll along the long narrow path.
Amateur fishermen strewn along the pond's edge
Sitting on boulders with kids on their shoulders;
Throwing their lines and making a pledge
To catch something, anything that will take the bait.
They just sit, and wait, and wait.

(3)
    But their greatest wish is to catch a fish
Then throw it back in for a duck's dish.
For those who cannot fish, instead
They bring to the pond scraps of bread.
Then they sit along the banks in ranks
Of children on the frontline, then their parents
While the seniors take their places on the bench.
As the ducks are being fed
You can greet the brown, spotted loons that glide along
Like a band of soldiers marching off to war.
Ever so often, one will break line to fly, but not very far.

You can intercept a photographer who's about to click
As a group strikes a pose with their ice-cream to lick
Under the trees just being kissed by the early Fall hue
Beneath a cloudless sky, beaming a perfect blue.

(4)
    As you round the bend on your left and right
You will pass tall thickets of overgrowth in sight,
Then wonder if they are tents being set up for rent.
Fallen tree logs that is home to termites and vermin;
Then you come upon sunken patches where folks have been
Many small clearings in the tall grass have been tested
Indicating that here, several lovers may have rested.
Soon you approach the wooden, planked bridge
Firm and sturdy - but only two abreast;
Built atop the musty, mossy, murky pond,
This one is likely to have some quicksand.
The water looks like green or maybe brown,
But so dingy and dirty, no creatures make any sound.

(5)
The air around here is a degree or two cooler
As lacking is the sun's penetration through the dense growth.
Pedestrians walk along – flip, flop – their slippers snap;
Clomp, clomp, the sound of shoes to the planky ground.
Hear the rhythm as the cyclist's tires go thud-op, thud-op
As they ride over the parallel spaces between the wood.
Or hear the stroller's wheels as they go bump, bump
Over the bridge made of the wooden tree stump.
Then hear the contrasting sound of the dog's toenails
As they peck, peck, against the wooden surface.
It is best to watch your step upon these planks
Or befall the same fate – where her stiletto shoe sank
Between the cracks and crevices in the wood
As you stroll along the Pond called 'Too Good'.

September 2007

BONA VISTA

Stressed, worn out and spent
Off to the Bona Vista Spa I went;
Where the Queen Suite
Is most heavenly for a retreat.

Decorated in burgundies, pinks and greens
Such tasteful colours lend to pleasant dreams.
With gardens of herbs and acres of rolling hills
There is lots of space for your exercise drills

The hostess opened her home to me
Where I welcomed peace and tranquility.
I will be back for another visit
Since this place was quite exquisite.

Thank you, Bona Vista
Thank you hostess for your hospitality.
This is not 'hasta-la-vista'
But back to the city I must flee

May you flourish in love and serenity
In the plains near Barrie, Ontario
Where fresh fruits and vegetables,
The local Farmers grow.

August 2006

CITY SIRENS

The city comes alive.
Pedestrians, passengers, cyclists
And those who drive
All wake up from daydreaming.
Eyes widening, hearts beating,
Blood pumping, pulse popping.

Temples thumping
As ambulance, fire truck and
Police cruiser speeds on by
With squealers on high.
People scampering
Cyclists pedaling
Motorists accelerating
Or stopping, as the case may be.

All hurrying to give way in emergency.
A driver gets stuck in traffic.
The siren bears down
Almost touching his rear bumper.
The siren WHIRRS
He whimpers
His leg shivers
His hand shakes

Where should he go?
He is surrounded.
Everyone! Please!
His dilemma you must ease.
Vehicles shift and squeeze
Finally!
He nods with a sigh of relief.

Now, the wailing vehicle is free
To speed, lead, go at will
To protect, prevent and provide
The city with contentment.
Adding a whole lot of thrill
And a touch of excitement
To the rush hour drill.

****

October 1999

FLOCK AT THE DOCK

Sitting by the South East Harbour
On the Boardwalk stretch
There dived many, many sea gulls,
Their daily lunch they must fetch.

As the peaceful blue waters lapped
The rusty rocks and soil,
From the blazing hot sun
I had to recoil.

I donned my sunshades and cap
And threw my purse from off my lap.
None too soon, I looked up to see
A flock of hungry birds, chasing one
That was awfully lucky.

How similar to the human race!
We all must share this earthly place.
Our body temperatures akin
Hair or feathers cover our skin.
They too must share this ocean space.

We both adapt well to warm weather.
We love to fly, and down south we go
To run away altogether,
From winter, cold, ice and snow.

Then from each other, we steal
Sometimes only a meal, sometimes more.
The comparison is unreal
And that is for sure, for sure.

....

August 1994

Green Gables
Cavendish
Prince Edward Island

GOOD BYE, P.E.I.

So here I am, leaving P.E.I.
This fair land, the apple of Canada's eye
For these past two glorious weeks
Will stay in my mind's eye for keeps...

As I hopped off the Royal Canadian Flight
I grabbed my luggage with all my might
On a scorching hot, sunny Saturday
A grand day being July thirtieth, my birthday

I stood outdoors feeling lost and alone
In a strange land, like a dog without a bone
I saw a taxi pulling along
With the driver whistling a merry song

A school teacher he was, an Islander
Quite happy to drive me over yonder
With a couple sharing in the rear seat
The female too, shared a birthday, neat!

Amazing combo-colours, rust, blue and green
The earthiest colours of which I am so keen
Of sky, sea, soil and vegetation
Who could ask more of any nation?

Taken to the Islander Motor Lodge
From staff and guests you could not dodge
'Cause you were very often called by name
Would think you were about to make fame

But fame you could not awaken
For Lucy Maud Montgomery had already taken
Being the most famous Canadian Author
A proud land that birthed a great daughter

To hospitality homes, guests are welcome
With cordiality, and then some
Such stopover I call a 'beddy'
Where beds are provided, but no 'brekky'

Folks visit Cavendish and Green Gables
And ride the Red Double Decker with no cables
Through manicured patchwork of green acres wide
Where blue skies meet the rolling turquoise tide

Much sights to see and places to go
Harbour Front, Harness Racing, Equestrian Show
Exhibition, Home Week Parade, time well spent
Or stop for rest and shade under the bingo tent

Alas! Now I must go
My plane leaves for T.O.
And so, with a great sigh
Goodbye, P.E.I.

~~~~~~~~~~~~~~~~~~~~

August 1994

JOLLY 'JOE'

Seated by the Confederation Centre Of The Arts,
Downtown P.E.I.
Engrossed in her crossword puzzle.
Joe, in a four-wheeled chair, stopped on by
For she - he was about to bedazzle.

She then asked, "Why are you sitting there,
While I am sitting here?"
To which he responded, "An accident
Some thirteen years ago,
The day that my car was totally bent".

So now he appears quite simple
Thirty-seven, independent and well groomed
Because at twenty-four, young and impossible
Straight into the ditch he zoomed.

Being drunk in a high speed chase
He told her that 'that was the case'.
"You beautiful black girl sitting here all alone?
An apartment I have, and would like to take you home".

She accepted his compliment with grace
As she did to many others before him
Then thought, 'They all have great taste',
And parted with her head a-soaring.

....

August 1994

THE PARK

The Park
An unpredictable place it is.
I came here for some peace and quiet
But instead I found a pleasant riot
Of kindergarten kids;
Wearing their summer costumes
Of tee shirts and tanks; shorts and pants
And some in the dandiest little skirt
Like tropical birds in rainbow plumes.
If I sit and watch them long enough
Soon, they will all be covered in dirt.
My reading and writing I must put aside
To watch the little cuties climb the slide;
Racing to and fro, back and forth
As they screechingly scream and shout;
Kicking the ball, over which they fall
And playing games of hide and go seek
Behind the evergreen being used as a screen.
Soon the monitor's whistle blows - tweet, tweet
Now they form in groups
Then march away in little troops.

The Park
An unpredictable place to which I came
It is now empty and quiet again
Yet, the perfect place to sit and watch the rain
From under the shed where I sat and read
Peaceful and quiet again - too quiet
And too dark, way too dark
The night creatures are starting to stalk
I must now leave the Park

~~~~~~~~~~~~~~~~~~~~~~~

August 2001

WRITING ON THE WALL

Written on the wall,
      As we strode through Ole Spanish Town
On Old Market Street
      In the burning, hot summer's heat.

The writing appeared near Martin Street.
      My daughter thought that this was neat,
So she fetched her camera, quick
      Before we could count to one, two, three,
The next sound we heard was, click!

      Upon developing
All of her film
      This is what we read, "....."
Then a thought came into my head.
      To spread a message of peace and unity
Is always good for the community.

      So, tell me Sire -
Is this your plan, your desire
      To light the Town and the Land afire
With unity, love, hope and peace,
      The likes of which should never cease?

"…..This is a plea from the Abiola Foundation.
   The Willie Lynch Syndrome
Has taken hold of our family.
   Black people destroying black people.
Worse than slavery.
   Divided we are the loser, mourner,
Uneducated, unemployed,
   Community undevelop.
United we stand strong.
   Together we can create school,
Jobs, opportunity, better community,
   Better Town.
Let us unite, not fight…."

By 'Unknown'
~~~~~~~~~~~~~~~~~~~~~~~~.
September 2007

TALES IN POETRY

Family Woe
Live Evil
Picnic Puzzle
Snow Dove
Stay Awhile
The Stranger

FAMILY WOE

There was this great big mystery
That should go down in history
This story is one of old
And must not go untold

A black lady, who was kind and brave
Decided to marry the tall white knave
They would have, indeed, had a good life
If it were not for family fuss and strife

The lady, she had a bigot for a sister
The knave had one too, who was no better
Those in-laws would fuss and fight
Each believing she was always right

The knave and his wife had many off-springs
Whom they would nurture, and give nice things
The in-laws, with no children of their own
Spent their time fighting like dogs at a bone

Then one terrible day in December
The kids, they will always remember
Their father, an Overseer with a gun
Got angry, and accidentally shot someone

Alas! The gun went off by mistake
And his poor wife's life, it did take
He thought to put the gun to his head
With his beloved gone, he too, wanted to be dead

The siblings, they were spread far and wide
Their love for each other they kept inside
As they grew further and further apart
With their pain buried deep in their heart

They soon married and had children, too.
The story was passed down, so that gossip was not new
To the nieces, nephews and cousins
Who were scattered abroad by the dozens

This tale they all will read
Of the tall, white knave who was freed.
But lived a somber life without his wife
All because of family fuss and strife.

==================
March 1993

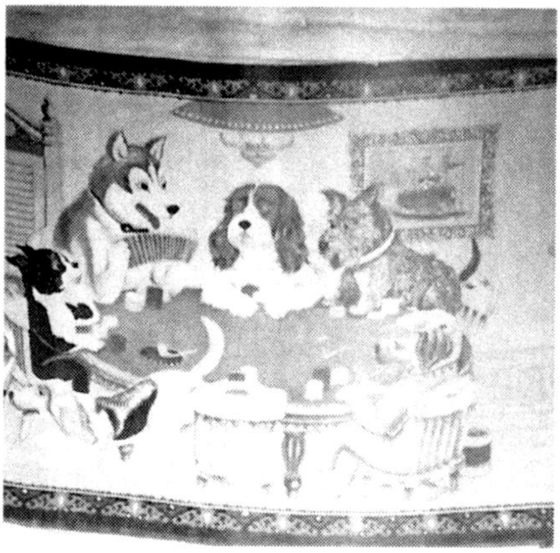

LIVE EVIL

Molly was a lover of pets
Or so the Townsfolk thought.
When they visited for afternoon tea
The animals would run wild and free.

Spouseless and childless as Molly was
She was never quite alone
She would breed the pets by the dozens
And later she sold them to her cousins

Molly took one pet down to the river bend
Stop! The rest will make you shiver
'Cause she tied a rope around its throat
And a rock she tied to the other end
While the pet wailed
Like a pre-slaughtered goat

She then twirled her pet like a lasso
Surpassing those cowboys at the rodeo
Then into the river she flung him
And stood to watch as he started to swim

But very far he did not get
For he sank lower and lower to his death
All because Molly knew
That this pet had chewed up her shoe

===================
March 2002

PICNIC PUZZLE

After a year of very hard work
When everyone from their duties shirk
To gather in laughter and good cheer
And to relax with a couple pints of beer

That was to be his day of fun
With friends soaking up the sea and sun
Then to his family he would return
His already brown complexion
Would show no signs of any sunburn

He left home on Saturday morning
Looking like dark honey
But was found the next day looking like ebony
It was dark at sea overnight
There was no trace of a tanning sunlight

What changed his colour? Was it poison?
That some alleged was slipped in his drink
And after a few sips, and a swim, it made him sink
Way down yonder into the vast abyssal
To bring about his end, so very dismal

Or pray tell about that dark mark on his forehead
Did the assailant use metal, steel or lead?
Then turned around to walk away
From the secluded area in the Bay

But upon hearing a slight moan and groan
And knowing that he was still alive
Grabbed him by a foot or a hand
And dragged him across the sand
To become fish food was to be his end

Alas! On the beach his body was found
No pulse, no life, not a single sound
Tell me how from his lungs no water they did see
When the Doctor performed the autopsy?

March 2000

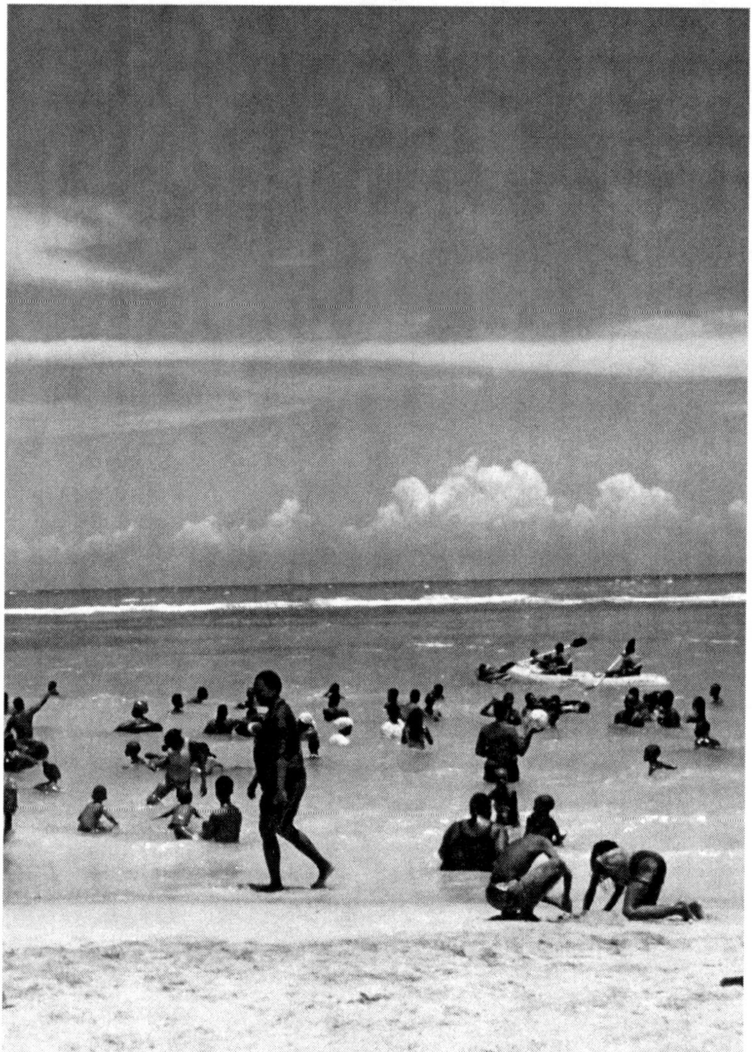

SNOW DOVE

Spring had already started, then halted.
Some snow had already parted
Leaving patches of green peeping.
But this patch was different.

Looking through the window pane
I did not want to see it again.
From the second floor,
It laid there motionless.

Laying there on one side
With its other wing spread wide
And its head flung back
And its eyes seemed shut.

Beak and feet were not obvious;
Or to this I may have been oblivious.
But very timid I was
To take another good look.

Poor thing! It must have fallen
An in the snow it became frozen.
Several very cold days passed by
And it was still untouched.

No disturbance from predators
Nor the lingering of any foul vapours
I should call the pest control
In order for it to be taken away

Instead, with my disposable bag and shovel
And a box of dirt and gravel
I decided to be brave and get close
Only to see a patch of snow
Formed in the shape of a white dove.

==================
October 2007

STAY AWHILE

Born in twentieth century, fifty
She was such a feeble thing
Helped others to be thrifty
As her talent was not to sing

Then came fifty-one hurricane
That almost blew her away
But the Lord, He said, "No way!
You were born and here to stay".

Now her mother who was not so bold
Sought the help of Auntie dear
Who sucked away that horrible cold
As baby turning blue was their fear

Well the fifties flew past
And she had a blast
With five other siblings by then
All six being born within year ten

Then came the sixties
Her folks well under their fifties
Gave them all a big surprise
A new baby bro' in front of their eyes

Now, with the seventies here
She too, is a mother dear
Of a bouncing baby girl
With hair unruly to curl

She took a holiday far and wide
With her daughter by her side
They survived the eighties
And are now in the nineties

And her little baby girl
With the stubborn lock of curl
Is just now beginning to unfurl
To find her way in her own little world.

`````````

March 2003
`````````

THE STRANGER

As the old man walked the streets
He was in a hurry to get there
He did not know where he was going
He only felt the need
A great desire to deliver a message
It was a message of doom and gloom
He must hurry, but where to
He kept on walking

The asphalt was piping hot in the parching sun
From a distance it seemed like steam rising
His shoes were beginning to wear
At the toes and the ball of his feet
Because that was where he mostly felt the heat
But he kept on walking

As he passed this particular house
He felt a vibration, a strong energy emanating from within
His eyes rolled over, he stopped, his hands clasped
His hairs stood on end, yet he was not cold
The goose bumps were like measles all over
His head felt light but larger than usual
He felt faint and was perspiring profusely
He stood there, shuddering

Yes, this is the house
He must warn her, him, them
He picked up a small stone from the roadside
His shaky hands were sweating
But he held on tightly to the stone
His eyes rolled over again
He knocked on the metal address plate
And waited

The dog, Bullie, rushed to the gate
He pounced, snarling and barking
The strange old man stood firm and eyed the dog
The woman came around the side of the house
She greeted him and asked if she may help him
He said no, he was here to help her
Could he have a word with her
She opened the gate and let him in

The dog held on to his pant cuff but he was not afraid
He had an important message to deliver
He snapped his fingers
The dog winced, lapped his tail between his legs and ran
She invited him inside and offered him a drink of water
He drank some, then wet his handkerchief and patted his face
He sat down on the chair which she offered him
Then she sat opposite at the dining table

Madam, I was sent here to deliver a message
I see death, disaster and disgrace in your family
You must go and get yourself looked after
There is a place I know where you can go…
Just then her husband came home
Upon seeing a stranger in his house
And hearing what he had to say
He decided to chase the old man away

A fortnight passed to the very day
In the same spot where she sat
By her very husband, she was accidentally shot

March 2000

VOCATIONAL VOICE

    An Adjuster's Jingle
    Comrades
    One Sixty Four

AN ADJUSTER'S JINGLE

When one is insured
For sure one is secured
From financial strain
Though they have nothing to gain.

With proper coverage
They will have leverage
And no doubt in their mind
That no hassles they will find.

Please don't be defensive
When reporting your claim
You are not being submissive
But just stating your aim.

To serve you, there are
Appraisers and Contractors
And other experts and advisors
Of your Adjuster, by far.

You declare you have injuries
And your vehicle is a wreck
You can't perform your duties
Oh! Where is that cheque?

You called the Lawyer, the Doctor
Physio and Chiropractor,
Because you will be laid up
For a long time after.

Be careful though;
Do be sincere and true,
Because you may never know
If the neighbour's watching you.

Those with petty nuisance claims
You ask if your premium grows
It depends on who is to blame
Only your Underwriter knows.

Your Adjuster has summed it all up
And wish you safety and good luck.
Take time to digest all this
Because it is written
'Without Prejudice'.

****

March 1993

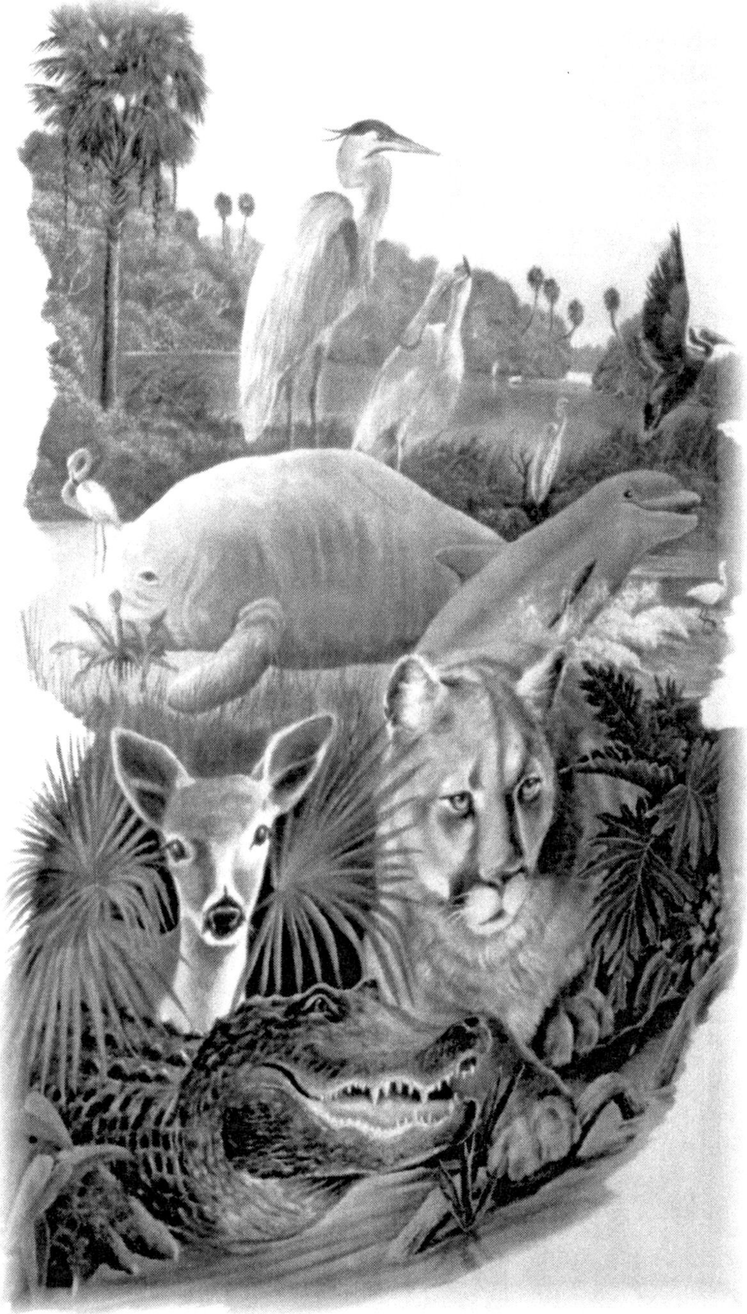

COMRADES

Mister and Mistress Insurer
How does your business grow?
Human Resources, Administration
Accounting and Underwriting
A definite no-no.
Look again, no mention of 'Claim'
This is your goal, your aim,
So your insured's respect, you will gain

And your reputation you will maintain.
In order to withstand the test of time,
Your soldiers you post on the front-line
The insured's first contact after a loss
They toil to keep clients from being cross
'Adjusters', they are called
Frequently threatened to be mauled
By clients who are appalled

At the imperfect service they receive,
While they wait, wait and grieve;
Feeling forgotten and frustrated
Hoping such incidents won't be repeated.
Adjusters, backed by a supporting staff,
These contribute to your clients' laugh
Personnel with experience and ability
To uphold your Company's philosophy

To produce, deduce and reduce through service
Your client retention being tops in the business.
Mister and Mistress Insurer, you who aspire
To be number one, this is your greatest desire.
You can turn your aspirations into bliss
If you are the innovator who will do this
Increase the personnel on your Claims list.
Remembering this is written 'Without Prejudice'

****

December 1997

ONE SIXTY FOUR

Again 'Without Prejudice'
I must tell you this
We now have Bill 164
And what a bonus of a score.

Since OMPP was not enough
We are into more bountiful stuff
With all of twenty parts
To fill their great big hearts.

We have a lot of forms and paper,
And our workload will be greater
With more clients to greet
And more deadlines to meet.

Some think this "Bill" is made in heaven.
From twenty parts there are eleven
And under these parts which eleven sits,
These categories all end in "benefits".

So let's review them all
That we may not take the fall;
For though we may know the truth
We must pay throughout the dispute.

"Income" and "Loss Of Earning Capacity"
For some, these can be tricky.
"Caregiver" and "Attendant Care"
For those who are bold to dare.

"Supplementary Medical" and "Rehab"
Most will feel good under SAB.
Check the "Maximum Limit" on above
And pay generously - with love!

"Education" and "Other Disability"
For those who are left in limbo.
"Death" and "Funeral" have our sympathy
'Cause after that, you have nowhere to go.

****

February 1994

PUNS AND JESTERS

Logo For Letterhead
New Dad
Pilot's Corner
Wedding Gift

LOGO FOR LETTERHEAD

Two primary colours of blue and yellow
They merge to produce a green so mellow.

Nature! So natural in all its splendor
Of these colours, I sat and wonder

Deep blue oceans, yellow sunshine and green trees
Hidden, but not forgotten, the Skipper oversees.

He steers us on towards greatness
With flying colours, and with great success

As we reach out to customers and vendors.
Achieving number one will soon be ours.

Others can now say that we have gained a lot
As we merge to form 'Avilot'.

October 2003

NEW DAD

Our Supe, Mister 'Thin'
Usually greets us with a smile;
One that could certainly beguile.
But now, he greets us with a grin,
And he will never be the same
Now that he has a new kin -

A daughter who will bear his name.
With his wit he keeps us jolly
Yet, our Unit shows no folly.
We are hard working as we jest
And by far surpass the Industry's test
Mister 'Thin' is a whole lot of fun

Especially when he jests with Ron.
When Supe is not being funny
He is saving the Company money
Through mediation, arbitration and litigation.
Mister 'Thin' is not only a funny laddie
He is a brand new, happy daddy.

October 2000

PILOT'S CORNER

The Skipper in blue
He whispers to you…
'Our Pilot, so strong and daring
Meeting corporate challenges and caring
For Brokers, Clients and Employees
And willing to make us all feel at ease
Personnel and clientele present and past
All know that our Pilot is here to last'
Where would you be without your Pilot?

The children are hungry
And the parents are angry
Their house is cold
Because the furnace is old
They called for service from the Hydro staff
'Simple, folks, your Pilot is off.'
You are secure when you insure with Pilot
Where would you be without your Pilot?

The Aviator is ill; could be the food
The plane is losing control, but not for want of crude
To 'Pilot', the Co-Pilot switches
And for the First Aid Kit he reaches
The crew and everyone is again safe
With the Skipper at the Helm
You can gain control when you insure with Pilot
Where would you be without your Pilot?

....
July 2000

WEDDING GIFT

Oh, heck!
I didn't check her size.

Well, it doesn't really have to fit;
This is just for having fun with.

Oops! Out falls her bosom
Out, into the hands of her husband

They are almost down to her hem
Can he handle them?

Here he goes with tongue and teeth
He nibbles at the strings.

They fall to her feet.
"Oh, how sweet" she sings,

"I just love these
Flimsy little things".

~~~~~~~~~~~
August 2006

MEANINGS

This is a collection of some words used in literature by Poets, Composers and Writers.

Alliteration:	a poetic or literary effect achieved by using several words that begin with the same or similar consonants, as in: Mary marched many meandering miles to the market
Allusions:	an allusion is an indirect reference to a person, place, thing, or event: The story contained an allusion to her childhood in Africa
Anacreontic:	written in the style or treating the subjects of the Greek poet Anacreon
Anapest:	a metrical foot of three syllables with the stress on the third syllable, or of two short syllables followed by a long syllable
Antistrophe:	the second type of metrical form in a poem that alternates two contrasting metrical forms
Assonance:	the similarity of two or more vowel sounds or the repetition of two or more consonant sounds, especially in words that are close together in a poem.
Ballad:	used in music or literature; a song or poem, especially a traditional one or one in a traditional style, telling a story in a number of short regular stanzas, often with a refrain

Bard:	a poet, especially one of national importance
Bucolic:	a poem about the countryside or country life
Canto:	a section out of several into which a long poem may be divided
Caesura:	a pause in a line of poetry, especially to allow its sense to be made clear or to follow the rhythms of natural speech, often near the middle of the line
Connotation:	the implying or suggesting of an additional meaning for a word or phrase apart from the literal or main meaning
Couplet:	two lines of verse that form a unit alone or as part of a poem, especially two that rhyme and have the same meter
Dactyl:	a metrical foot of one long syllable followed by two short syllables in classical verse or one stressed syllable followed by two unstressed syllables in modern verse
Denotation:	the most specific or literal meaning of a word, as opposed to its figurative senses or connotations
Dialect:	nonstandard spoken language
Dithyramb:	a passionately emotional speech or piece of writing
Doggerel:	poetry that does not scan well and is often not intended to be taken seriously; something that is badly written or makes no sense at all

Eclogue:	a pastoral poem, usually in the form of a dialogue between shepherds
Elegy:	a poem that mourns somebody's death
Epic:	a lengthy narrative poem in elevated language celebrating the adventures and achievements of a legendary or traditional hero
Fable:	a short story with a moral, especially one in which the characters are animals
Figure of speech:	an expression or use of language in a non-literal sense in order to achieve a particular effect. Metaphors, similes, personification, irony and hyperbole are common figures of speech
Foot:	a basic unit of rhythm in poetry, made up of a fixed combination of stressed and unstressed or long and short syllables
Haiku:	a form of Japanese poetry with 17 syllables in three unrhymed lines of five, seven, and five syllables, often describing nature or a season
Hexameter:	a line of verse that has six metrical feet, usually all in the same or a related meter
Hyperbole:	figure of speech using deliberate and obvious exaggeration for effect, e.g. I could eat forty million of these
Iamb:	a metrical foot of one short or unstressed syllable followed by one long or stressed syllable
Ictus:	the stress that falls on syllables in poetic rhythm

Idyll:	A short poem about rustic life; a scene or event of rural simplicity
Irony:	humor based on using words to suggest the opposite of their literal meaning
Jingle:	a catchy tune or verse, usually one that is played repeatedly to advertise something; to have a sound or rhyme that is catchy or repetitious
Libretto:	the words of a dramatic musical work such as an opera, including both the spoken and the sung part
Limerick:	a five-line humorous poem with a characteristic rhythm, often dealing with a risqué subject and typically opening with a line such as "There was a young lady called Jenny." Lines one, two, and five rhyme with each other and have three metrical feet, and lines three and four rhyme with each other and have two metrical feet
Lullaby:	a gentle song for soothing a child, especially into sleep
Lyric:	relating to poetry that often has a musical quality and expresses personal emotions or thoughts
Macaronics:	describes verse containing words and phrases from everyday language mixed with Latin, other foreign words and phrases, or vernacular terms with Latinate endings, usually for comic effect
Madrigal:	a song with parts for several usually unaccompanied voices that was popular in England in the 16th and 17th centuries; a short pastoral or love poem suitable for singing as a madrigal

Measure:	Poetic meter - the rhythm of a piece of poetry
Metrical Foot:	a unit of meter in poetry
Metaphor:	all language that involves figures of speech or symbolism and does not literally represent real things
Meter:	an arranged pattern of rhythm in a line of verse; the pattern of beats that combines to form musical rhythm
Monody:	theater in Greek tragedy, an ode for one actor to sing alone
Muse:	to ponder or meditate on; consider reflectively; in Greek mythology, one of nine daughters of Zeus who is the goddess of art; a source of inspiration in poetry
Narrative:	a story or an account of a sequence of events in the order in which they happened
Ode:	a lyric poem, usually expressing exalted emotion in a complex scheme of rhyme and meter
Onomatopoeia:	imitation of sound in words; the formation or use of words that imitate the sound associated with something, e.g. "hiss" of a snake, "buzz" of a bee, "sizzle" of bacon
Palindrome:	a word, phrase, passage, or number that reads the same forward and backward, eg: live evil; or 1234321

Pentameter:	a line of verse consisting of five units of rhythm such as five pairs of stressed and unstressed syllables
Personification:	the attribution of human qualities to objects or abstract notions
Poem:	a complete and self-contained piece of writing in verse, that is set out in lines of a particular length; and uses rhythm, imagery, and often rhyme to achieve its effect
Prose:	writing or speech in its normal continuous form, without the rhythmic or visual line structure of poetry
Prosody:	the study of the structure of poetry and the conventions or techniques involved in writing it, including rhyme, meter, and the patterns of verse forms
Purple Passage:	a section in a piece of writing that is very elaborate or contains too much imagery
Purple Patches:	a period of good luck or success
Quatrian:	a typically rhyming four-line stanza
Refrain:	something that is frequently repeated, e.g. a saying or an idea
Rhyme:	similarity in the sound of word endings, especially in poetry
Rhythm:	a particular pattern of stress in a poem or kind of poetry; the pattern formed by stressed and unstressed syllables

Rondeau:	a poem of 13 or 10 lines in 3 stanzas, with 2 rhymes and with the opening phrase repeated twice as an unrhymed refrain
Simile:	a figure of speech that draws a comparison between two different things, especially a phrase containing the word "like" or "as"
Sonnet:	a short poem with fourteen lines, usually ten-syllable rhyming lines, divided into two, three, or four sections
Spondee:	unit of poetic rhythm; a metrical foot of two long or stressed syllables
Stanza:	a number of lines of verse forming a separate unit within a poem
Stich:	a line of poetry
Strophe:	the first type of metrical form in a poem that alternates two contrasting metrical forms
Symbol:	something that stands for or represents something else, especially an object representing an abstraction
Theme:	a distinct, recurring, and unifying quality or idea
Tone:	the way somebody says something as an indicator of what that person is feeling or thinking
Triolet:	a poem consisting of eight lines with a rhyme scheme of abaaabab in which the first, fourth, and seventh lines are the same, as are the second and eighth lines

Triplet: a poetic stanza of three lines, usually with a single rhyme and sometimes sharing the same metrical pattern

Trochee: a metrical foot of one stressed syllable followed by an unstressed syllable

Troubadour: a writer or singer of love poems or songs

Villanelle: a 19-line poem, originally French, that uses only two rhymes and consists of five three-line stanzas and a final quatrain. The first and third lines of the first stanza are alternately repeated as a refrain that closes the following stanzas, and are joined as a final couplet of the quatrain.

REFERENCES

Words and meanings were found in the following:

1. The New American Roget's College Thesaurus, in dictionary form – revised edition prepared by Philip D. Morehead. Copyright 1985 by Philip D. Morehead and Andrew T. Morehead.

2. The American Heritage Dictionary of the English language copyright 1969, 1970, 1973, 1976, by Houghton Mifflin Company.

3. The Internet was also used for meanings and spell check.

ABOUT THE AUTHOR:

Veronica Moore was born in Jamaica, West Indies. Being from a large family and always surrounded by many friends and relatives, she acquired a real love for life and nature. She completed her education in Jamaica and was fascinated with English literature and writing. She migrated to Canada in the early seventies and gained more of life's experiences. This led to the culmination of these poems, and at last, she decided to publish her work.

Printed in the United States
143553LV00001B/11/P